CTW

SESAME STREET®

The Together Book

written by
Revena Dwight

illustrated by
Roger Bradfield

featuring Jim Henson's Muppets

The *Sesame Street Together Book* was created to entertain your child as he (1) tests his logical thinking by choosing the object that will prove useful in each set of circumstances, and (2) discovers that things go more smoothly when we cooperate with each other.

This educational product was designed in cooperation with the Children's Television Workshop, creators of Sesame Street. It has independent educational value, and children do not have to watch the television show to benefit from it.

Workshop revenues from this product will be used to help support CTW educational projects.

A SESAME STREET BOOK

Published by Western Publishing Company
in conjunction with Children's Television Wo

Copyright © Children's Television Worksho
Muppets Copyright © Muppets, Inc.
All rights reserved. Produced in U.S.A

GOLDEN®, A LITTLE GOLDEN BOOK, and GOLDEN PRESS®
are trademarks of Western Publishing Company, Inc.
Sesame Street and Sesame Street Lamp Post and Sign are
trademarks and service marks of Children's Television Workshop.

No part of this book may be reproduced or copied in any form
without written permission from the publisher.

D1226384

Fourteenth Printing, 1979

What do I have that needs a helper?
I have a wagon that just won't go. . . .

Who has something good for wagons?

WHEELS ARE THE NIFTIEST
THINGS I KNOW!

What do I have that needs a helper?
I have a double-thick malted milk. . . .

Who has something good for drinking?

DOWN IT GOES, AS SMOOTH AS SILK.

What do I have that needs a helper?
I have a hill piled high with snow. . . .

Who has something good for sliding?

ONE, TWO, THREE—
AND DOWN WE GO!

What do I have that needs a helper?
I have a cake that's going to fall. . . .

Who can keep the cake from falling?

LET'S SIT DOWN AND EAT IT ALL!

What do I have that needs a helper?
I have skates that won't stay tight. . . .

Who has something to make them fit me?

GOOD! NOW LOOK!
THEY FIT JUST RIGHT!

Every day I need a helper.
Every day you need one, too.
There's so much we can do together. . . .

YOU HELP ME, AND I'LL HELP YOU!